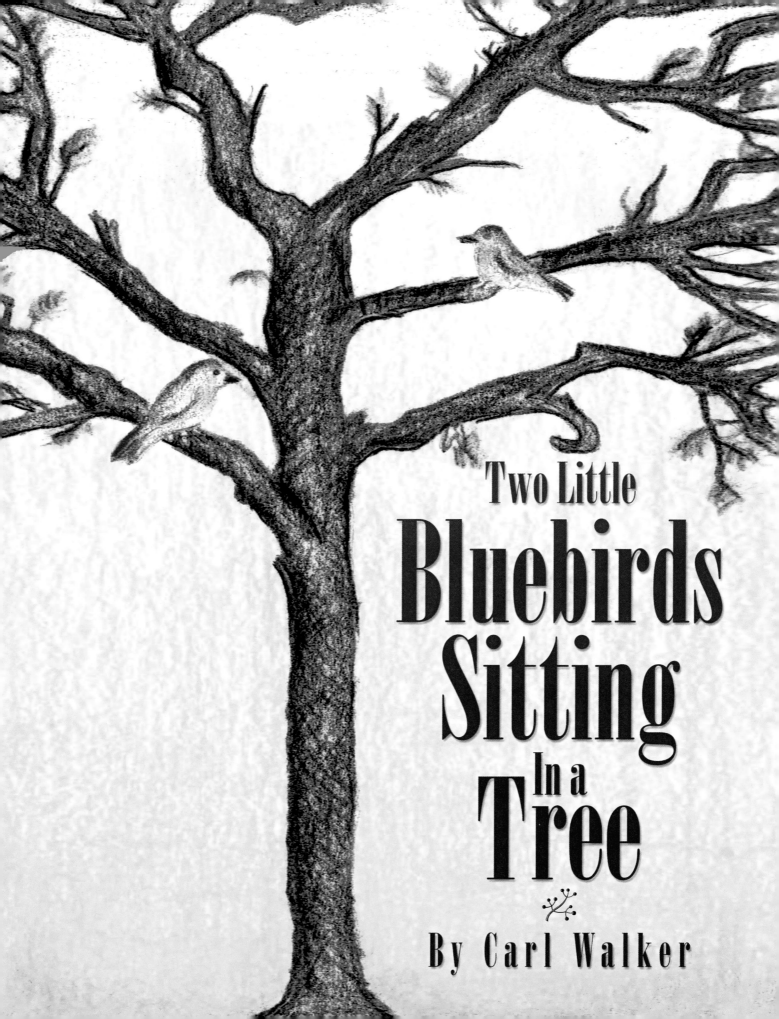

Two Little
Bluebirds
Sitting
In a
Tree

By Carl Walker

AuthorHouse™ LLC
1663 Liberty Drive
Bloomington, IN 47403
www.authorhouse.com
Phone: 1-800-839-8640

Published by AuthorHouse 02/14/2014

ISBN: 978-1-4918-4555-4 (sc)
ISBN: 978-1-4918-4556-1 (e)

Library of Congress Control Number: 2014901974

I would like to dedicate this book to my wife, Nancy, for her support and encouragement, and to my granddaughter, Samantha Walker for her lovely, professional illustrations which add so much to the book

TWO LITTLE BLUEBIRDS SITTING IN A TREE

Two little bluebirds sitting in a tree top singing,

"I love you. Fly away with me to the moon light chapel."

Mr. Cardinal sits on his branch. "Bluebirds welcome to the moon light chapel. Nancy Berry Miller will you take Carl Gordon Walker and fly away for life?"

"Yes. I love you."

"Carl Gordon Walker will you take Nancy Berry Miller and Fly away for life?"

Mr. Cardinal sitting on his branch, "By the power invested by heaven's open window and the bright stars and mars, I pronounce you bluebirds husband and wife."

The stars are brightly shinning. The whippoorwills and the ocean waves are whispering, "I love you sweetheart. Place your hand in mine and kiss me all night long."

LIGHTING FLASH

Sparrow, Hawk, Swan, Owl, Peacock, Turkey

Mr. Hawk says "We are going to have a big party – and much earthly food and water – on the 10th day of Hawk in the year of happy flying feathers—and all of our fine feathered friends are welcome."

Red birdy says "Who of our fine feathered friends is getting married? Sparrow and Hawk? No."

Mr. Hawk says. "The same kind of bird. The whisper is that it might be red bird, turkey, or quail."

Mr. Hawk says "This will be big. We must tell everyone to wear their best – and be sure and clean your feathers three times."

The day of thunder and lightning: Mr. Quail said, "It's going to rain".

Mrs. Turkey says "No, Just beautiful, sunshine and clear skies. So we may dip in the birdbath before the wedding."

The day is full of excitement. "Who will she be?"

The birds wedding song: Birds of a feather always flock to gather. Singing together will it be three redbirds in a nest. Will it be an eagle or three?

Mr. Turkey says, "Flying eagles will lead the way. Miss Peacock waves her feathers at all of her fine feathered friends and stands beside her Peacock, her only sweetheart."

Mr. Turkey says, "To my fine feathered friends, we are gathered here on the 10th day of Hawk in the year of Happy Flying Feathers."

Mr. Turkey says, "By the Gobble, Gobble invested in me, I pronounce our fine feathered peacocks husband and wife."

WILL SHE KISS ME?

Will she kiss me under the tree?

Will she kiss me in the rain?

Will she kiss me in the snow?

Will she kiss me on the mountain?

Will she kiss me in the valley?

Will she kiss me in the barn?

Will she kiss me near the river?

Will she kiss me under the stars?

Will she kiss me under the mistletoe?

Will she kiss me at the alter?

Will I say I do?

Will we live happy ever after?

STAN GETS MARRIED

Rita and her family move to Kansas. Stan is dating Betty Sue. She is just 4'10", thin and very pretty. Stan and Betty Sue get married on the 4th of July. The church is across the road from Dad's 5,000 acre farm. The weather is perfect. A nice cool breeze and many friends come from far and near. The church has a gable roof and stained glass windows. The bride walks down the long winding stair case, the flower girl follows, and the ring bearer behind her. The lights are down low. The maid of honor, the bride's maid and ushers follow.

At the farm all is ready. Many tables are set. The food is ready. In the big barn, all is ready for music and dancing, after the wedding service. Everyone goes to dad's big barn. Rascal Carl is standing by a big tree. Thinking: "Oh my. "Oh yes!!! Pigs, chickens, ducks, and one cow. Oh Yes, the goat!!!" Everyone has sat down to eat. The dancing and the music and the singing are going great.

In the barn Ray said, "Is that a duck I hear?" The pigs are in the barn running all around. On the dance floor, the chickens are flying on the tables. The old cow is knocking over the tables. The pigs are helping themselves to the food on the ground. The people are running and crying. The goat is running into the bride's table. What do you think dad did to Rascal Carl?

WHAT IS LOVE?

Is it a kiss, a handshake?

Is it from the heart? A dozen red roses?

Is it helping with the kids, washing the dishes, washing the clothes, moping the floor, respect – honor, loyalty?

Can it be bought with gold?

THE FROGS GO TO CHURCH

On Sunday May 10th, mother's day, Bob is to preach his first sermon. He was the talk of the town. Two weeks before mother's day, Rascal Carl goes down to the river to listen to the birds, and frogs. Rascal Carl said, "I will teach the frogs to sing." Now on mother's day, May 10th, there were hundreds at the church service. Rascal walked into the church service with two frogs in his suit coat. He sat behind Betty Thomas. She loved to sing very loud. No one would sit on either side of her. Rascal takes from his pocket two frogs. When the next song starts, Rascal will put one on each side of her. The frogs begin to sing: Croak, croak, rebit, croak, croak, rebit, croak, rebit, rebit.

TWINKLE TOES

She twinkles in the morning

She twinkles in the sunlight

She twinkles under the stars

She twinkles by the moonlight

She twinkles in the evening

She twinkles in my heart

THE FUZZY BROWN BEAR

A long time ago six brothers and two sisters lived on a farm. There were pigs, horses, cows, chickens, and ducks. There was Stan, George, Bob, Jim, Ray and Carl and sisters Mary Martha and Barbara Ann. Carl was the smallest, so mom called him Rascal Carl. He did not like to share any toy.

Dad went away for one week to help a friend on his farm. Barbara Ann said, "Look Jim. Dad is back." Barbara Ann said, "Dad Rascal Carl will not let us play with big brown fuzzy bear."

Dad said, "OK"

"Daddy, Daddy. I am the smallest. Jim and Bob are bigger than me."

Dad said, "Mom has been sending me notes about how you do not share any toy or big brown fuzzy bear". After Rascal finished washing the dishes and mopping the floor, Rascal goes to the front room, where all of his brothers and sisters are playing with all of the toys and big brown fuzzy bear. Dad said, "Go to bed now."

On his way to his bedroom, he said, "I will always share all of the toys."

The next morning Rascal ran down the stairs and jumped into his Dad's lap and said, "Dad I will always share all of the toys and big brown fuzzy bear." Rascal ran outside singing, "I will always share all of the toys all of the time with all of my brothers and my sisters." Rascal Carl lived happy ever after.

WILL HE BE MINE

Will he talk to me?

Will he kiss me?

Will he hold my hand?

Will we look into the blue yonder?

Will we sail the ocean blue?

Will we look at the twinkling stars?

Oh yes! Will he be mine?

Will he love me?

Will he be my sweetheart and

Love me all the time?

THE REBEL SONG

Verse I

Rascal Carl was young.

Now he is crazy and old.

Only he is our general.

Now when you see two red birds in a tree and the butterflies waving like a crocked Road, you know we will win.

Verse II

Now when you want brains we look to Carl.

He puts all the things in the right order.

That is why those yanks cannot win.

Verse III

So we have rascal, crazy, and brains on our side.

We always win! Win! Win!

The Battle of Beaver Creek 1865

The union command—General Washburn with 75,000 men, his staff, Major Paul Baker. Captain Steven Jacobs, 1st Lt Vernon Winchester.

Southern command-General Rascal Crazy Carl, Major Parker.

The battle of Beaver Creek takes place in West Virginia. The union is on the south side of Beaver Creek, with 75,000 men. The Union is ready with lots of food and ammo. The Union scouts hunted and killed deer. They have made beef jerky. They have captured a large plantation with a garden.

Black Bart rides into the Union headquarters at 10 am May 5th, 1865. He said, "May I see your general in charge." Black Bart enters General Washburn's tent. He and all his staff are talking about the upcoming battle.

He says, "Have a seat Black Bart and tell me about this crazy general we are about to take apart and where are those rebels?"

He said, "Five day's march away. First let me tell you, he is crazy and a rascal. 2nd before the war Rascal rode up and down the Mississippi River gambling on the boat. One time he tricked me in a card game. I lost two million to him. The next day we went fishing. While we were fishing, he said, "I have something you lost yesterday. Come over to my horse and look into my saddlebag. Be sure and count the money." He had given me back one million. He said, "You must be more careful. You may never know who will deal you a bad hand. He was a slick and clever card player.""

1st Lt Steven Jacobs said, "May I tell you about Rascal? My unit, the 158 Infantry was at Billy Goat Gruff valley. We had thousands of rebels running and we captured 2,500. Crazy Rascal turned thousands of goats on us. They ran all over our units. We were lucky to get off the battle field."

2nd Lt Vernon said, "May I sir"

He said, "Tell your story."

"I was in the 6th Calvary at Goffer Crossing. Our horses ran hard and fast after those rebels. Only after 30 minutes our horses started to fall. Those gophers ran all over the place. We wasted more ammo on those gophers than we did on those rebels."

Sargent Ray Peterson pocked his head in the tent and said, "May I sir? This will be the last story. I was with the 8th Calvary. We had those rebels pinned down. There was no place for them to go. It was almost dark, when all of these butterflies came in front of us by the hundreds. We could not see anything. When the butterflies stopped flying, there were no rebels. They had taken the dead, wounded, weapons, ammo, stopped firing – It was dark and they had slipped away. It was spooky. Not even an old owl made a sound."

General James Washburn, "No more of this Rascal Crazy Carl, that worthless rat and pig. When he arrives I will show him what real men can do."

Colonel Lancaster said, "General Sir. I do hope you know what you are doing, because you are in for one big surprise. On the 9th of May the 67th Calvary division of Rattle Snakes from the 9th army slid across the river and put 24,000 union soldiers asleep. They have a special venom that puts a man to sleep for 12 hours. The beaver raiders brought up hundreds of red ants to get into the yanks food supply and give the yanks all kinds of problems."

Black Bart goes back across the shallow side of Beaver Creek to make a deal with all of General Washburn's staff except Colonel Lancaster. He gives each staff member $50,000. They each said thanks to Bart. "We are going home tonight."

May the 10th, the union forces are ready. Their 100 cannons are pointed in all directions. The Gatling gun crew is pointed to the right flank. Pickets are out guarding both sides. General Washburn said, "Colonel Lancaster you did a good job setting up our defenses."

He said, "That Crazy Carl will come up with his crazy plan."

The general said, "I have only beaten him two times. Look four red birds in that tree."

Colonel Lancaster said, "Yes sir. Hold on to your seat. He is going to hit hard and fast."

What General Washburn does not know is that 24,000 yanks are fast asleep for six more hours. Black Bart paid the 500 union pickets to leave and his staff except Colonel Lancaster. Then a division of butterflies are waving like a crooked road. The rebels have let lose 1,000 fox jumping at the union line. The yanks start firing at them. The red ant division starts running up the pant legs of the union force. Then 500 rebels start firing down at union forces from the tree tops. Then, 3,000 cavalry charge from the right flank. The union has no place to go. With 1,500 infantry charging behind the cavalry, General Washburn said, "What are we going to do? Surrender, I suppose. Not me! You coward"

Just as General Washburn gets on his horse. Three wasps, 4 hornets, and 6 bees from the rangers 22 division of the 7th army sting General Washburn's horse at the same time. The horse falls dead.

The general is trying to get up, Crazy Carl says, "Some fight. Hand over your sword, General Washburn." All union prisoners are taken off the battlefield.

DARLING GARDENIA

She is my precious gardenia.

She is my sweetheart.

I have prostate cancer.

She did not shut the door on me.

She did not fly away into the wild blue younder.

She did not sail into the ocean blue with another.

She holds my hand.

She kisses me under heavens stars and moon.

She is so kind, sweet, pretty, gorgeous, and thin.

When I cry she holds me tight in her arms.

She is my darling gardenia.

When I hear her name, my heart flutters.

Her eyes sparkle like the stars in the sky.

WESTERN ROMANCE

Characters

Jackson Samuel

June

Katie Thomas before marriage

Katie Jones Married

Chuck Jones—sheriff

Bull Dog Frank—bandit

Mary Jo Nurse

The Clinton gang

Mr. Johnson Samuel's dad

Sheriff Tom

Chapter I

Samuel Jackson is born in Wilcox, Arizona March 13th, 1798. He is an only child. His dad, Matt Jackson is a big rancher of 40,000 acres. In 1812 Samuel is fourteen. His first girlfriend is Cee Ann Weeks. He goes over to her home in the summer of 1812. He takes her for a buggy ride. They go down by the river and have a big picnic. When they arrive back at Cee Ann's home, her dad says, "Young lady get off that buggy and get in this house." Her dad said, "You are not going with this worthless kid. You must court a real man." Samuel is standing there shaking in his boots. Her dad says, "Kid, rat, punk get off my land before I shoot you."

Cee Ann says, "Dad please he is nice. Those other boys treat me so bad."

By the time you could count to twenty, Samuel was out of sight. He said, "Oh dear Lord. Thanks for saving my life and for her dad not shooting me." Samuel told his friend later, "I do not know where she went. Only I did not love Cee Ann."

In September of that year Samuel was courting Bernita Elmore. Samuel goes to pick up Bernita – Only Alvin Ham was already at her house. She says, "See you later sonny boy. We are going for a buggy ride." And three weeks later she says, "Alvin is going to take me for a real romantic moonlight boat ride. You have not ever done anything romantic like that with me. I saw you and Cee Ann on your buggy ride. I also heard her dad ran you off. Now Alvin is a real man. He knows how to romance me. Not only that we are going to get married the next day. Not only that, I told Alvin we are not going to invite you to the wedding. Bye Bye."

In 1816 Samuel says to his dad, "I am sixteen. I am going to Kansas on a cattle drive with the triple X ranch." When he arrives in Kansas City, he goes to the Wild Horse Saloon with the other cattlemen. There were twenty dancing ladies. Only there was just one pretty young lady. Later after the dance, Samuel goes over to meet the young lady. He said, "I am Samuel Jackson. I am here with the triple X ranch cattle drive. Will you please come over to my table, so we may talk?"

She says, "Yes. I am Katie." She said, "I do not like that hard stuff they drink."

He said, "I do not either." He said, "There is a river nearby. So we may go for a buggy ride and a picnic?"

She said, "Yes. I know the perfect place. Pick me up at 10:00am in the morning."

They go for their buggy ride. They come back three hours later, so she can get ready for work. Just as they get back to town, there is a big shoot out with Sheriff Jones and Bull Dog Frank's gang. Bullets are flying all over the street. When it is over, four cowboys lay dead from the stray bullets. The sheriff Jones is wounded and Katie is hit in the side.

Samuel Jackson says to Bull Dog Frank, "If Katie dies; I will hunt you down and kill you myself."

Katie is taken by the buggy over to the doctor's office and placed on a bed. The doctor says, "It does not look good."

Samuel says, "Doctor she has lost so much blood."

Mary Jo, the nurse, walks into the room. She says, "Not bad. I have seen worse."

Samuel says, "The last time I saw you, you hit me over the head with flowers I had given you. You said you did not love me and ran off with that army man."

She said, "It was for the best." Samuel says, "Doc here is $5,000 I won in a little card game a few days ago. Take care of my darling sweet Katie." He said, "I just meet her. Only I know she is not going to live". He rides off into the sunset.

Back at the doc's office, it was touch and go – This means some good days, some bad days with Katie's health. Ninety days later, Katie is getting much better. Katie says to Mary Jo, the nurse, "Where's that nice cowboy that brought me to the doc's office? He was nice and kind, so sweet he was."

Mary Jo, the nurse, said, "Oh that no good cowboy. He courted me a few times. He was always crazy."

Four weeks later the Sheriff Chuck Jones comes by to visit Katie. He said, "That was some gunfight. I am lucky to be alive. I am OK now." He also said, "All of those cowboys from the triple X ranch went back to Wilcox three days after the gun fight. Katie, if that cowboy had not brought you to the doc's office you would be dead."

Chuck said, "Will you marry me?" She said, "Yes." "Oh Katie I have a small ranch here—only dad wants me to go to Wilcox, Arizona and help him with his large ranch."

Katie says, "Is that a promise. And you will give up that badge?" One week later, Chuck turned in his badge; they were married, and catch a stagecoach to go to Wilcox, Arizona.

Samuel is at the train station in Benson, Arizona, when he sees a beautiful young lady. He walks up to her, "My lady, would you be Nancy?"

"Oh! No! Are you the Samuel that ran off into the sunset, when dad, Joe, and that navy guy was helping WJ fight those Indians?" She said, "If it had not been for Joe and his sharp shooter we would be dead."

Samuel said, "I was scared they would scalp me."

She said, "You would be better off dead."

Samuel says, "What ever happened to your navy boyfriend?"

"I am going back to Texas to get married to my Navy man. I hate this place." Nancy said, "I can hear the train a coming. It is just around the bend."

Samuel says, "Oh! My! May I ask you one more question? Will you marry me? I know your train will be here soon. Oh! Just a few years ago I was in Kansas. I bought this wedding ring. I was going to give it to someone else. Only when I and my girlfriend arrived back in town there was a big shootout in front of the bank. Fifteen or twenty died that day. My girlfriend Katie was shot. The doc said she would live. Only I did not believe him. So I rode into the sunset. I can hear the train about three miles away." Samuel got down on his knee and he said, "Nancy I am scared."

Nancy said, "Oh! No! I am going to get married to a real man that is not scared."

Samuel goes back to his dad's big ranch to work for him. When Samuel arrives home, his dad says, "I know your heart is set on working the ranch. Only I have a big surprise for you. There is gold in our nearby creek. Preacher parker is going to take in a load of gold for us in the morning. I want you to hold back a short distance because of Bull Dog Frank and the Clinton gang." His dad was also thinking Bull Dog and his friends would be off robbing banks and trains.

On the morning of February 20th, Reverend Parker, his wife Mary and their son are on the way to the Valley Bank with the gold. Samuel is watching the preacher turn the corner with the horses in full fun. He said, "We have a problem because the preacher does not like a fast moving wagon. Tim Clinton slips behind Samuel, knocks him off his horse, ties him up, takes off his boots, hangs his rifle and pistol in a tree just about five feet high. Tim ties his horse near a stream. He knows if he just lets the horse go Samuel's dad will go to the sheriff.

Bull Dog Frank and the Clinton gang stop Reverend Parker. James Clinton says, "What is your hurry, Mr. Preacher Man?"

Mary,, his wife says, "Run Son. Jump now."

Bull Dog says, "You were the pretty little dancing lady at the Crazy Horse Saloon a few years ago. Your mom shot my horse to death after she found out we had hung your dad and burned your house. Now that was after we stole everything from your home."

Mary said, "I have changed my life. We are going to heaven when we die."

Tom Clinton said, "You are wrong little lady." He drew both six shooters and shot Mr. Parker and his wife Mary Parker ten times.

Louis Clinton said, "I know where the bag with the gold is. Only take the gold out and dump it."

Bull Dog says, "No! Leave the gold in the bag." The grand take from Mr. Parker and his wife was 20 pounds of gold. Bull Dog Frank said, "I want us to go to our hide out near Mexico."

On February 23 Bull Dog Frank is a short distance from his hide out in Green Valley. A Mexican gang member rides up to Bull Dog and said, "I am Carlos. I know where we can find some good gold in Mexico just across the creek. Mexico is going to have a big fiesta. Many pretty dancing ladies, much food, drinks, singing. I will see you there on the twenty-fifth. We will talk and party."

Three cowboys ride into Wilcox on the twenty-fourth of February. They go to the sheriff's office and tell him that they were looking for their lost cattle. Only what they found was a wagon, two horses they shot because they were almost dead and one man and woman shot many times. The sheriff Tom, three cowboys and doc ride back to the wagon to pick up the dead bodies. When they arrive at the wagon, Samuel walks down the hill in a daze. He said, "What's going on." He said, "Oh! No! Dad's gold, and the parkers are dead." He said, "Reverend Parker and his wife were on their way to town. I saw the wagon turn the corner at a full run. Then someone came up behind me and knocked me out." The three cowboys go on their way back to their ranch. The sheriff, doc, and Samuel take the parkers back to town.

Chapter II

Samuel works on his dad's ranch for 2 more years. Then on March 16ᵗʰ, 1818 he goes to church on Sunday. He meets Katie after service. He said, "I gave you up for dead and I rode off into the sunset."

She gave him a great big hug and said, "I know. I was not sure I was going to live myself."

Samuel said, "What ever happened to Mary Jo?"

Katie said, "Her husband was scalped by the Indians. So she married a captain in the army and they went off to Texas."

Katie said, "Do you remember June?"

Samuel said, "Yes. Where is she?"

Katie said, "We're going to have a big barn dance next Saturday at 1:00pm. She will be there."

Samuel said, "I will be there. See you next Saturday at 1:00pm."

The next Saturday at 1:00pm Samuel was at the barn dance. Katie said, "this is June one of my dear friends. She helped my get back on my feet when I was shot in Kansas."

Samuel said, "May I have this dance?"

She said, "Yes." They danced for a long time. She said, "Let's go get some food and punch."

Samuel said, "OK."

She said, "Let's go down by the river for a moonlight walk."

Samuel said, "I am going on a cattle drive one more time. June, may I court you when I return?"

She said, "Yes! Yes! Yes!!"

Samuel goes back to Kansas for the second time, with the triple X ranch cattle drive. When Samuel arrives in Kansas, he goes to the Black Horse Saloon to watch the dancing ladies and play cards. A young lady went over to Samuel's table. She said, "Do you remember me?

He said, "I think so."

"My name is Cee Ann." Cee Ann said, "Do you remember Katie? She said, "Yes. Bull Dog Frank told my dad you shot Katie and you shot Bernita and Alvin Ham's boat nearby. He said you also shot their horses and you also burned their home while they were at church."

Samuel jumped to his feet, "That no good worthless Bull Dog lied."

"Samuel, my Dad said I must never court you or he would kill both of us. Just last week Bull Dog and Dad got in a gun fight over some gold my Dad had taken from a nearby creek. He shot my Dad and he died in front of this saloon one week ago. Today he said what are you going to do now? My friend is a major in the army. He is off fighting Indians. When he gets back we are going to get married and go back to Maryland." She said, "What are you going to do?

I started going to church where I met June. She is so sweet. We went on a moonlight walk just before I left on the cattle drive."

She said. "You never went on a moon light walk with me or a buggy ride."

Samuel said, "It was your mom."

She said, Oh! Yes! My mom would lock me in the back room every time she saw you coming. Oh! Yes! She had a window in that room. Just so I could see you coming. I cried so many times. She also said you were no good for me."

Samuel said, "Let's go for a moonlight walk tonight. I know you are going to get married and so am I. Let's just take this one moonlight walk for old times."

She said, "Oh! Yes! This will be great." She said, "May we also hold hands?"

He said, "Yes."

Samuel goes back to Wilcox, AZ to help his Dad and marry June. Samuel goes over to June's home in a buggy. She sees him coming.

She runs outside. "You're home. I have some bad news for you. Your Ma and Pa were killed by the Clinton Gang while you were gone."

He gets off the buggy and goes over to his Ma's chair on the front porch and starts crying. He said, "Ma and Pa will not get to see me get married to June. You will marry me, won't you?"

June says, "Yes! Yes! I love you. I want to be your wife."

He jumps for joy. "We will have the biggest wedding in town." He said, "First we must go to the sheriff Tom and see if he knows where the gang might be."

She said, "My sister Judy is going to get married in 3 weeks. She is always pulling pranks on every one."

Samuel said, "I have a great idea for her. I wrote a story for my brother one time about two frogs going to church. I will tell you the story. This will be a great prank on her."

Samuel and June went for a buggy ride the next day and a picnic down by Silver Springs Creek. After that they rode back to town to buy her new clothes for the wedding. Just before they arrived in town, Sheriff Tom rides up and stops Samuel and said, "Bull Dog and the Clinton Gang are in town shooting up everything."

Samuel said, "I will take my extra horse that is tied to the back of the buggy. June, please, take your time going to town. Sheriff, you and I will take the short cut to town. We will go in back of the bank." When they arrive, there are five cowboys hiding behind the bank.

Samuel goes slowly around the bank so he can see what is going on and who is near the front of the bank or who is inside the bank. Just as the Clintons came out of the bank with the gold, Tim Clinton said, "This bank job was easy." Then three cowboys opened fire on the horses. No one gave up. Samuel opened fire from one side of the bank and the sheriff opened fire from the other side of the bank. Two cowboys ran out of the saloon and finished off their horses and the Clinton Gang. All of the Clintons lay dead alongside their horses. Bull Dog walked slowly out of the bank with his hands up. The sheriff walked around the other side of the bank so he could see what was going on. Samuel said, "You cowboys come with me. Fifteen cowboys and the Doc take the horses out of town."

June runs up to Samuel, "Are you OK, my dear?"

He said, "Thanks to my Dad for training me how to shoot from the time I was a kid."

Bull Dog said, "Sheriff I do not give up. Where is that Samuel Jackson? He is no good just like his Mom and Dad. I tell you sheriff; I will stay in jail two days. I must have a duel with him. If I shoot him dead, you will let me go free and I will never ever come back to this worthless town forever."

The sheriff said, "OK. Today is Tuesday. We will have the shootout Thursday at 1:00pm."

Bull Dog said, "OK."

Samuel told June, "I will have a duel with Bull Dog in two days."

She said, "Will you be the better shot? "

He said, "My Dad showed me a few tricks. I will show you on Thursday." The word is out: Bull Dog and Samuel Jackson will have a duel on Thursday.

Everyone far and near go to town and line the street from one end to the other. Also a Texas Ranger is there, a marshal from Tombstone, Tucson, and Benson. There were many bets on who would live or die. Sheriff Tom lets Bull Dog out of jail and gives him his six-shooter. The sheriff walks out first, then Bull Dog. The three go to the middle of the street. There is not as much as a whisper from anyone. The sheriff stops and says, "OK Samuel stop and get back to back. I'm going to count to 20. Samuel and Bull Dog start walking. The sheriff said, "1, 2, 3, 4, 5, 6, 7, 8, 9, 10, 11, 12, 13, 14, 15, 16, 17." Samuel stops and turns left then a quick right turn. He fires two shots and hits Bull Dog between the eyes, before Bull Dog can pull one six shooter and fire one shot. There are many happy cheers, hand claps, and many of the folks are happy the Clinton gang is gone, besides he and his game had killed at least three hundred people and robbed many banks and trains. June runs up to Samuel and gives him a big hug and kiss.

The four lawmen walk over to Samuel and said, "Thanks. It is over. Over four hundred have died because of those thugs. You will receive a large reward from us."

Samuel said, "Thanks men. Whatever amount I receive for the reward, I will keep one-half for myself and the other half will go to my church so the church can help the loved ones that have been hurt by those thugs."

One week later June's sister gets married. Samuel waits until the preacher starts to say, "Rita, do you take . . ." and he takes the frogs out of his coat pockets and they say "Ribit! Ribit! Ribit!"

After the wedding, Rita said, "Samuel that was some prank you pulled on me."

June said, "I did not know his crazy prank. He never did tell me what it was."

Three weeks later, June and Samuel get married in Wilcox, Arizona at the large First Southern Baptist Church. Everyone is seated. The music starts. The flower girls drop the flower petals down the aisle and June follows in her lovely wedding gown. The wedding party is standing in front of the preacher. He said ladies and gentlemen we are gathered here for this young couple to get married. Katie raises her hand. The preacher said, "I forgot. We have some special friends from the past here." Cee Ann and her husband, Katie and her husband, Bernita and her husband, Carol and her husband, Mary Jo and her husband walked down the aisle and stood behind the wedding party. The preacher went on to say, "Samuel, do you take June to be your lawful wife to have and to hold for life?"

He said, "I do."

The preacher said, "June do you take Samuel to be your lawful husband to have and hold for life?"

She said, "I do."

He said, "You are now husband and wife."

SWEETEST

Sweet Heart

Sweeter than red wine

Prettier than red roses

Heart More Precious than gold

Eyes sparkle like the stars in heaven

Texas Ladies

Characters:

Ora Mae Parker

Richard Parker

Gordon Joe Parker

Judy Kay Kelley

Barbara Ann—Hair Stylist

Valerie Nichole—Dress Maker

Aleta

Gordon Joe Parker is born in New York July 19th, 1858. His Ma is Ora Mae Parker. Mr. Richard Parker was a major in the union army. Feb 8th 1865, he walks into his house. He said, "Ora Mae let's go to Dallas Texas."

She said, "Are you sure?"

He said "yes! My brother is a big rancher in Dallas, Texas."

She said, "A family can get a train ticket for $3.00 to go from here to Dallas, Texas this week"

Gordon Joe said, "Oh yes! Pa let's go now.

On Feb 25th, 1865, Mr. Richard Parker and his family go to Dallas, Texas by train. So on March 2nd they arrive at Dallas Texas. His brother meets them at the train station and takes them to his ranch. His Ma became a Sunday school teacher, and played the piano, and directed the puppet show. His Pa became the new youth preacher at their new church in Dallas.

So on March 10th Gordon Joe starts to school. Kids in Texas school Call Gordon Joe – City Slicker Gordon. One week later he is walking to school, when he sees three white and black animals. He takes a stick and starts poking them. He gets sprayed by all three skunks. At school that morning all the kids said here comes City Slicker Gordon. The teacher rings the bell and all of the kids run into the classroom and sat down. City Slicker Gordon is the last one in the classroom. Just as he walks in the door, the kids jump up and turn around and say Stinky Gordon. From that time on he is no longer called City Slicker Gordon. The kids now call him Stinky Gordon.

Aleta told some of the boys, "Let's play a prank on Stinky.

"They said, "What do we do?"

Aleta said, "Every Tuesday he buys flowers for his Ma and his Pa is helping, Tom, Mr. Parker's brother, round up cattle."Aleta and the three girls go over to Ora Mae's house. She is reading her Bible.

The girls ask, "What are you reading?"

"The Bible" she said.

The girls say, "Gordon is so sweet and kind to us. He brings us wild flowers, and sings to us the sweetest songs."

Ora Mae said, "I know he is so sweet and kind and he does have the sweetest voice."

The boys are just outside the front door setting up a little trap for Stinky Gordon. Aleta goes over to the kitchen window and said here comes Stinky on his horse. All of the kids run to the back yard and wait on Stinky. Stinky gets off his horse and goes up to the steps. He walks up on the porch and said, "Ma I brought you a dozen purple Lillis."

She said, "Thanks Gordon." Just as he opens the door to take the lilies inside, he slips on the small toe trap. The water from the vase falls all over his Ma's head. The lilies fall on the floor. The vase breaks in many pieces.

Stinky goes over to the hair stylist salon and said, "May I mop your floors and clean your windows?"

Barbara Ann said, "Yes. I do need some help in this place."

Stinky waits until the ladies come in for Barbara Ann to work on their hair. He brings in two buckets of frogs and lets them out. The frogs start jumping all over the floor, ladies, and windows.

Barbara Ann said, "Get Out of here rascal!"

For the next two years, he helps his Ma and Pa playing, riding, learning how to play horse shoes. He also stayed out of Barbara Ann's Ladies Hair Salon.

In 1873, he is now fifteen, his Ma is teaching the youth boys and girls how to put on a puppet show. On April 17th, 1872, Easter Sunday, Judy Kay and her Ma and Pa came to church because they heard that there was going to be a puppet show about Jesus on the cross. After the morning service was over, everyone came up to Stinky Gordon and said what a good job he did with his puppet.

Judy Kay's parents came up to him, "You did such a good job. Will you come to our house and have lunch?"

Her Pa said, "I hear that you are good with horses and horse shoes."

Stinky Gordon said, "Yes sir. Will you take me back home before dark?"

Mr. Kelly said, "Yes, young man."

Judy Kay walked up to Stinky Gordon and said, "You did a good job with the puppets. I am going to tell all of my friends we cannot call you Stinky anymore." She said, "Will you walk with me so we can go with Ma and Pa for lunch?"

He said, "Yes. Gordon and Judy Kay get in the buggy with her parents and go to their home for lunch and to play horseshoes.

The next Sunday many people go to church. The preacher said that in three weeks the puppet show will be Jesus feeds the 5,000.00. After the morning worship service, Gordon ran up to his Ma and Pa and asked, "May I invite Judy Kay over for lunch today? Then you and her Pa can play horseshoes. After lunch, then Ma and I can show Judy Kay how to make the puppets work."

His Ma said, "Tell them to come right over." Gordon went over to Judy Kay's parents, and said, "Mr. Kelly may Judy Kay ride to the house in Ma and Pa's wagon?"

He said, "Yes, sir, young man."

On the third week everyone enjoyed the Preacher's message and the puppet show about Jesus feeding the five thousand. Two weeks later after the morning worship service, there was a large picnic, horseshoes and contest who could catch the biggest fish.

It was now 1875, Gordon is seventeen and Judy Kay is eighteen. It is early May 1875 and there is a large barn dance. The dances played were the waltz, and square dance.

Barbara Ann tells Aleta, "I am not happy with Gordon."

Aleta said, "What do you mean Barbara Ann?"

Barbara Ann said, "That little rascal cost me hundreds when he pulled that frog prank on me."

Aleta said, "I was out of town when that happened. Only I do remember when that little rascal put a dead rattle snake on my back porch. It was all coiled up and looked like it was alive. Also that same afternoon, he brought up a bucket of ants and put small amounts of fish in the bucket."

Barbara Ann said, "Let's fix this today, now."

Aleta said, "I have heard that he wants Judy Kay to marry him, only he is too scared to ask her Ma and Pa so they can get married."

Aleta said, "I have the perfect idea. You and I will go up to the ladies from his schooldays and say Stinky Gordon do you remember our moonlight walk? Do you remember the picnic? Do you remember the ice skating?"

Barbara Ann said, "Oh! Yes! This will be fun."

Gordon and Judy Kay are dancing the waltz. Then the two ladies went up to Gordon and Judy Kay and each sang a short song. " Do you remember dancing, moonlight walks, fishing by the moonlight in the summer, riding the stagecoach to look out point, ice skating, riding horses, playing horseshoes, taking a moonlight ride on the riverboat, holding my hand and our first kiss, holding your hand and looking at the moon?"

Judy said, "We need to go sit down and have a talk. You said I was the only one."

He said, "Please, my dear, please listen to me. I know who is behind this. Aleta is. When I was young and before I was 15, I killed a rattle snake and put it on her back porch all coiled and made it look like it was alive. Then, I went to the front porch with a big bunch of ants and a small amount of fish while they were gone. And for Barbara Ann, I asked her if I could work and clean her hair salon. She said yes. So I took two buckets of water, waited about 1 hour, waited for all of the ladies to come in, then I dumped water and frogs at the same time.

It was so funny. You should have seen all of those ladies jumping up and down and Barbara Ann coming at me with that big mop."

Judy Kay said, "Let's dance some more." Gordon said, "First my lady let's eat and take a moonlight walk."

She said, "OK".

June 1st 1875, Gordon and Judy Kay take a buggy ride down by the river. They stop for lunch and listen to the birds sing.

Gordon says, "You are so sweet, pretty, my darling. Will you marry me?"

She says, "Yes, my sweetheart, when?"

He said, "July 26th at 3:00P.M." He said, "This will give you and Valerie Nichole time to make your wedding dress. I also want her to make a dress the color purple, tan, and gold. On July 12th, two weeks before we get married we are going to the biggest hotel and have an all-day meeting with all of our friends."

Judy Kay wears her new purple, tan and gold dress to the hotel. Gordon says, "We are going to have a large Texas style breakfast, lunch and supper."

She said, "Who is going to pay for all of this?"

He said, "Me and Pa. We just found a large amount of gold in a stream near the ranch. We have already built a large two story house for you and me. There are small trees and a stream, so you and I can take moonlight walks and our kids can run and play after we are married."

She said, "How did you know I would say yes?"

He said, "I have been praying ever since I saw you in church on that Easter Sunday and God answered my prayer."

On the 12th of July, Gordon and Judy Kay went to the big hotel in Dallas to meet with many of their friends, to eat, play horseshoes, and fish, and take walks by the lily and rose garden. On July 26th, at 3:00pm, Gordon and Judy Kay get married. She has a lovely white wedding dress and a ten foot long white train. The young flower girls scatter purple and white lily petals. They live happy ever after.

THE WILD WEST

Preti-near I was a cowboy.

Preti-near I was a gun slinger.

Preti-near I was a bank robber.

Preti-near I was a gambler.

Preti-near I was a banker.

Preti-near I was a sheriff.

Preti-near I was a singing cowboy.

Preti-near this poem is preti-near not the truth.

STAN THE GENERAL

Stan is home from the three year war. He was the youngest general in his unit. At the age of 23, he is now in the front room of his dad's house, telling his war stories, with many family members and friends, also his girlfriend Rita. This is February 18th `1832. Rascal Carl and mom are in the kitchen fixing popcorn. Mom tells Rascal to take a big dish of popcorn into the front room. Rascal is walking into the front room. When he enters with the popcorn, he says, "Hi, general and hi Betty. You look so sweet."

Just as Rascal is getting ready to put down the popcorn, Stan says you little rascal and takes off a shoe. Mom walks in the front room just in time to see a shoe flying, popcorn flying, and her best dish flying into 100 pieces, and Rita jumps up and down slapping Stan. "You told me I am the only one, and your only girlfriend. You sent me letters telling me how sweet I am." She runs out the door slamming it so hard it was hanging on one hinge.

Mom walks over to Rascal and says, "Are you OK Rascal?"

A Cowboy's Dream

Cowboy sitting next to chuck wagon – He looks up to the shining moon, and says, "I wish I may dream up on this star tonight – with the brightest shinning moon." He sees 20 pretty dancing ladies. So nice and kind – a Dark cloud moves over the bright shining star. He said, "Those pretty ladies where are they?"

The dark cloud clears. The beautiful lady says, "Hold my hand. Come with me. Let us go down the dusty trail. Let us sing: Dear Lord, thank you for taking us through the rain storms, muddy roads, over the mountains, keeping the Indians away, the bandits too. Let us go before the preacher man and say I do so we may walk down the dusty trail for life hand in hand".

MY SISTER BARBARA ANN

My sister Barbara Ann – small and pretty. I gave her a duck. It said, "Quack, Quack." She is seventeen.

When she was sixteen, Mom went to Mrs. Jones and asked her to have a birthday party for Barbara Ann at her house because Mom is going on a big business trip and will not be back on Sept 7th, 1948 for Barbara's birthday party. Mrs. Jones said yes.

In Sept of 1947 Rascal Carl goes to the river to listen to the birds and frogs. While he is there, he meets his friend Tommy Toe.

Tommy Toe is a mouse friend of Rascal's. Rascal Carl said, "Can your sister Katie sing?"

Tommy said, "No and why do you ask?"

Rascal Carl said, "I want her to sing at my sister's seventeenth birthday."

Tommy said, "I can teach her to sing."

In two weeks Rascal Carl goes to Mrs. Jones' house and asks her, "May I see the candles for my sister's party?"

She said, "Yes Rascal."

He says, "Mrs. Jones those candles are drab. May I bring you mine before the party?"

She said, "Yes."

So at 2 P.M. Sept 7, 1948 Barbara Ann's seventeenth birthday party is at Mrs. Jones house. Barbara Ann blows out the first candle.

Rascal says, "What is wrong with that thing? He counts, "1,2,3,4,5,6,7,8,9,10,11,12,13,14,15,16,17."

Frosting from the cake goes all over Rascal Carl, Barbara Ann's new dress, Mrs. Jones new table and couch.

Rascal Carl said, "It was only a small candle"

Tommy and his sister Katie go to the party, so Katie can sing a special song for Barbara Ann, "Down by the river and out by the barn, I can hear the animals sing-moo, cluck, ribbit, quack, quack, quack, moo, ribbet, cluck, quack, cluck, cluck, quack, moo, moo, ribbet, ribbet."

KEANU THE NAVY MAN

Keanu the Navy man

Handsome and tall

Smart of all

The ladies bow – Mr. Keanu Navy man

Please be mine

To have and to hold.

My heart floundered,

My heart melts when I see you

In your navy blue

Please hold my hand

And kiss me all the time

Be my sweetheart all the time.

JERRI LYNN'S CHRISTMAS STORY

The Main Characters Are:

Susan (in real life Jerri Lynn)

Her Mom Betty Lou

Her dad Thomas Joe

Three sisters:

Mary Jo

Judy and

Carol

Three brothers:

Bill

TJ

Tim

Other Characters:

Rascal Carl

Boots the cat

Squeaky the mouse

Mr. Jack Rabbit and his wife

The frogs

Mr. Rabbit and his wife

The hound dog patches.

Jerri Lynn's Christmas Story

One summer afternoon Rascal Carl asked all of his animal friends to come to the fishing pond, so they could talk about Susan. Rascal arrives at the fishing pond with Patches at 11:00am. At three all of his friends showed up. Mr. Jack rabbit says, "what are you thinking of?"

"You see Susan has a birthday on December 24th and her family always has a big Christmas party on the 25th of December. May I have the help of all of my friends that are here today?"

All of them said "Oh yes. Oh Yes". Rascal Carl said, "We will meet back here one week from today and make the Christmas plan."

Susan comes home from school on Friday and said, "Mom and dad may I have Rascal Carl come over for my Christmas birthday party?"

Bill Jumps up from the table. "Do you remember when Judy had her first date? He was hidden in those big rose flowers. He poked his head out and said "Judy your slip is showing"".

Just then Tim walks in. "Do you remember when he put blue bugs in T.J.'s blueberry birthday pie?"

Susan says "Oh Stop, Stop. Mom, Mom please, please!!"

Her mom Betty Lou says "OK yes".

Her Dad, Thomas Joe says "Oh No" to himself. "I know that Rascal Carl. He is planning a big trick on all of us."

The morning of December 24th Susan was jumping up and down. "Rascal Carl will be here for my Christmas party. I haven't seen him for 5 years". That night after supper, Dad, Thomas Jo, pushed himself back from the table. "Betty Lou your supper was great. I think that will hold me, if we have an early breakfast. OK Kids time for bed. Santa will be here soon. We must all be tucked in asleep."

Just as everyone is getting ready for bed, Squeaky and Boots said "we must let everyone go upstairs. We will give them one hour to go to sleep."

Squeaky said "do you remember the plan?"

Boots says "yes." Now Bill has for his present a Navy Boat. Tim has a train. TJ has a baseball hat and a catcher's glove. Mary Jo has a ragged Ann doll. Judy has earrings and necklace all in silver. Carol has the tea set and play house. Susan has a DVD player, computer and a Christmas Dress.

Boots and squeaky slip in under the Christmas tree and they put the girl's

things in the boy's packages, and all of the boy's things in the girl's packages except for Susan's package. They hid her original gift and put a package under the Christmas tree filled with dog toys for Patches. The old hound dog is sleeping nearby.

Boots says to squeaky "Old Patches will not say anything he was fast asleep." There is just one problem. Patches was only being very still and watching everything, just as Boots and Squeaky go out of the room, Patches goes up the stairs and tells dad everything.

Dad said, "Thanks Patches". Then dad said to mom, "I am not going to tell the kids." Ten minutes later Tim and TJ are sliding down the large stair case banister.

TJ says "Look Santa left cookies and red roses for Mom." A short time later, Mom, Dad and all of the kids are by the Christmas tree.

Dad said "Do you remember one year the boys are first and the next year the girls are first? This year the girls are first." Dad says "OK Susan you are first."

Susan says "Oh Mom I know what this is. You always wrap the gifts so nice." She slowly opens the gift. "Oh no Dad, dog toys for patches."

Mary Jo is in so much of a hurry, she rips the paper. "Oh no – a train".

Carol says, "Oh I know Rascal Carl. He is so kind and sweet he always wraps my gifts so pretty. What is this?"

Dad says "a navy boat play toy." Dad says, "OK Judy."

Judy says "I am not sure I should open this gift. Oh no. That crazy Rascal Carl, he knows I hate baseball."

Bill says, "Dad do I have to open my present?"

"Oh yes son, now."

He opened his very slowly—"Mom, a ragged Ann doll! What am I going to do with this thing?"

T.J. said, "This is crazy. What is in this package for me?"

Judy says "Open my brother and you will find out."

He slowly opens the gift – earrings and a silver necklace.

Tim says, "Must I open this thing?"

All of the girls joined in at the same time, "Oh Yes!!"

Just as he starts to open his gift Patches, Boots and Squeaky come around the corner just in time to see him open his tea set and play house. "Oh no, wait until I find Rascal Carl." The kids started laughing and changing gifts. And Boots and Squeaky give Susan her original gift.

Right after gift opening time and gift exchange, they have lunch and went in by the fireplace. Rascal Carl drives up in his car with the frogs and rabbits. He walks to the door and Boots and Squeaky let everyone in. Boots and Squeaky go in the other room and get the record player for the music. The frogs and rabbits jump and hop on the piano and the music starts. The frogs are doing the waltz and the rabbits are doing the polka. Bill says look Rascal Carl's friends are dancing on the piano. Susan comes up to Rascal Carl after all of the music is over. She gives him a big hug and says "Thanks and Merry Christmas. She said I kind of know you are a little crazy. Only I love it."

A Sailor's Dream

Standing here by the ocean waves, I am looking into the bright moonlight.

Oh dear Lord who will it be?

Will she be tall?

Will she be short?

Will she be pretty?

Will she be thin?

Will she be a red head?

Will she be a brunette?

Oh dear Lord will she say I do?

Will we sail into the sun set?

BLUEBERRY PIE

Once up on a time, six boys and two girls lived on a big farm in Missouri. Stan, George, Jim, Bob, Ray, and Carl were the boys. Mary Martha and Barbara Ann were the girls. The smallest was Carl. He was always playing pranks on everyone, so mom called him rascal. Mom was in the kitchen making cornbread. Mary Martha and Barbara Ann were playing with their dolls. The boys were in the barn playing. Rascal walked into the kitchen with a small cup. He said, "Mom what are you making for supper, anything special?"

"Oh yes, cornbread and blueberry pie."

He said, "Look at the pretty red bird Mom."

Mom was taking a long time looking out the window and telling Rascal all about the red bird. In the cup he had some blue bugs. He put the blue bugs in Mom's pie mix. After supper, Jim said, "Mom this is the best blueberry pie you have ever made."

HEAVEN'S OPEN WINDOWS

Sergeants never cry

Heavy heart

Sorrow

Sadness

Tears running like a river

Sergeants get out of the valley

Go to the mountaintop

Lift your eyes to heavens blue sky

Why Oh, My

Mary Martha, Mom, Dad, Stan, Ray, Nancy

And Jim

Standing in heavens open windows

Sergeants never cry

MR. SQUIRREL GOES TO CONGRESS THIS IS A FICTION STORY WITH A REAL LIFE MEANING

Let's give my friend and yours a very warm welcome. All creation stood up and gave Mr. Skunk a 5 minute standing ovation.

Mr. Squirrel says to Mr. Black, "Will you please tell the group why we are meeting today."

Mr. Black Bear says to his creation friends, "I have been talking to The Tree Huggers Conservatory. They want to make the San Pedro River a nature refuge from Hayden to Benson, Arizona. This means one mile on each side of the river, many miles of fencing, to keep the humans from fishing and hunting."

Mr. Chicken Hawk said, "I flew over the Walker's chicken house. You see that is no big deal."

Mr. Wild Pig, "I can run under the fence."

Mrs. Mountain Lion, "I can take one graceful leap and go over the fence."

Mr. Bull said, "Me and my beautiful will be fenced in forever."

Mrs. Rabbit says, "I can run and jump those fences. It is no, big deal to me."

Mrs. Frog says, "I can hop and run wherever I please."

Mr. Squirrel said, "Are you ready for a vote?" They all say yes.

Mrs. Frog said, "I want to make a motion: The Tree Hugger Conservatory cannot set a plan for a nature preserve or set up a flood plain one mile on each side of the San Pedro River, Hayden to Benson, Arizona. The BLM must pay a fair price for this land. If this deal goes sour then the homeowners will only get pennies on the dollar."

Mrs. Chicken Hawk said, "I will second the motion."

Mr. Squirrel said, "We are all going to Gulf Port Mississippi on Swan Airways. We will all stay at the Beaver Creek Lodge, from July 4th until the 8th. We will have more time to talk about this motion and have fun in the sun. Our wives will have time to go shopping and visit. Mr. Black Bear and his friends will pay all costs."

July 4th everyone is having supper at Beaver Creek Lodge dining hall. Mr. Squirrel said, "Be here at 1:00pm July 8th so we can vote."

July 8th Mr. Squirrel said, "Are you ready to vote?"

Everyone jumps up and down and says, "Yes! Yes! Yes!"

What say you Mr. Skunk? "Yes".

What say you Mr. Black Bear? Yes.

What say you Mr. Rabbit? Yes.

What say you Mrs. Frog? Yes.

What say you Mr. Chicken Hawk? Yes.

What say you Mr. Wild Pig? Yes.

What say you Mrs. Mountain Lion? Yes.

What say you Mr. Bull? Yes.

Mr. Squirrel says, "The motion is carried seven to zero. Thank You. We will be flown home by Peacock Airways. This is at Bluebird Ave. and Red Bird Street. Mr. Lizard Limousine Service will pick you up and take everyone to the airport. Mrs. Frog and her friends will pay for your flight home."

COWBOY'S PRAYER

Cowboy is lying on the ground looking up to heaven on this moonlight night. He says, "Dear Lord I have been a gambler, train robber, gunslinger, banker, and a sheriff. Oh dear Lord please forgive all of the things I have done badly. I want to marry the pretty lady from Kansas and have a large ranch in Texas". Cowboy goes sound asleep under the stars. The Lord shouts "Wake up cowboy! Wake up! I will forgive you of all of your bad ways. I will also grant you your second request. You will marry the pretty lady from Kansas. Also you will have a large ranch".

Cowboy's Thank You.

I stand here on the Texas plains. "Dear Lord, thank you for my wedding queen from Kansas. Thank you for the green fields far and near. Thank you for the water and all of the cattle. Last, but not the least, dear Lord, thank you for saving this cowboy and my bride, so we may live in heaven ever after".

FOR FORBIDDEN LOVE

Will she kiss me in the sunlight?

Will she kiss me in the moonlight?

Will she kiss me under the stars?

Will we walk hand and hand on the beach?

Will we walk hand in hand down the dusty trail?

Printed in the United States
By Bookmasters